RIDGEWAY MIDDLE SCHOOL ANTHOLOGY

CHANGES

RIDGEWAY MIDDLE SCHOOL ANTHOLOGY

CHANGES

Sharon J Hall, Editor

iUniverse, Inc.

New York   Bloomington

This is a work of fiction. All of the characters, names, incidents,
organizations, and dialogue in this novel are either the products
of the author's imagination or are used fictitiously.

iUniverse books may be ordered through booksellers or by contacting:

iUniverse
1663 Liberty Drive
Bloomington, IN 47403
www.iuniverse.com
1-800-Authors (1-800-288-4677)

Because of the dynamic nature of the Internet, any Web addresses or
links contained in this book may have changed since publication and may
no longer be valid. The views expressed in this work are solely those of
the author and do not necessarily reflect the views of the publisher, and
the publisher hereby disclaims any responsibility for them.

ISBN: 978-1-4401-4773-9 (sc)
ISBN: 978-1-4401-4774-6 (ebook)

Printed in the United States of America

iUniverse rev. date: 05/19/2009

CONTENTS

——— CHANGE ———

MS. KATHERINE PATRICK'S CLASS

Ms. Deborah Dyson's 8th Grade Language Arts Class

MUSINGS

MRS. DYSON'S STUDENTS

DR. PRECIOUS BOYLE - SOCIAL STUDIES

Mrs. Givinia Causey - Seventh Grade Clue

——————LETTERS TO SHARON DRAPER——————

DR. PRECIOUS BOYLE - HOMEROOM
AND
MS. SUSAN FERRARA'S - LANGUAGE ARTS STUDENTS

Ms. Mahalia Davis - Language Arts

Mr. Ken Greene's General Music Students
My Vision of the Future

Mr. Ken Greene's General Music Students
Music

MISCELLANEOUS MUSINGS

INTRODUCTION

It's these changes in latitudes, changes in attitudes;
Nothing remains quite the same.
With all of our running and all of our cunning
If we couldn't laugh, we would all go insane.

Jimmy Buffett

We all have big changes in our lives that are more or less a
second chance.

Harrison Ford

Things do not change; we change.

Henry David Thoreau

As we have done every year since the 2005-2006 school year, students at Ridgeway Middle School have worked together this year to create a book filled with their thoughts, their imaginings, their joys, their sorrows, and their fears. This year's book, even more than the earlier editions, reflects the *CHANGES* our students have experienced in their young lives.

This year, the Roadrunners have watched in wonder as a beloved coach strives daily and heroically against a dreadful illness. They have come together in grief as a teacher, new to the school but completely embraced by her students, passed. Some students come from families hit by the current recession. Already financially challenged, some families have experienced job losses and pay-reductions. Some families have been forced to move without warning, left homeless by foreclosures.

It has also been a school year of unexpected joy: Americans electing our first African American president; teachers welcoming eagerly-awaited babies; Roadrunners being accepted into the new International Baccalaureate program at Ridgeway High School.

For all, the end of this school year and the beginning of the next will bring changes. This year's eighth graders will be promoted, becoming ninth graders in the fall. Staff members who have graced our halls for years will leave to accept other assignments, and new teachers will fill those spots in August. Ridgeway Middle School will become an optional school, seeking International Baccalaureate membership in 2010.

As we complete this school year and embrace whatever CHANGES life brings, this volume will help us understand those who helped us become the people we are...and the people into whom we will CHANGE.

Linda S. Simmons

Administrator Emeritus

Change is inevitable – except from a vending machine.
Robert C. Gallagher

FALLING STARS

In Loving Memory of Amelia A. Bartholomew

By: Lexus C. Stafford

Many years ago, Grandma June made a lovely quilt for a little girl named Elizabeth. On the quilt, she stitched falling stars with long tails and Elizabeth's name. She loved the quilt her mother had made for her. She sat with the quilt wrapped around her and watched the dark sky for falling stars. Elizabeth loved to have tea with her dolls on the quilt. Sometimes she accidentally spilled tea on the quilt. Sometimes, Elizabeth pretended the quilt was a dress and she wore it when she rode her toy horse. Once, the quilt was torn but her mother repaired it for her. Elizabeth loved to play hide-and-seek with her sisters. She would hide from them under the quilt. Her sisters always knew where to look for Elizabeth. Whenever Elizabeth was sick, she would sleep under the quilt and it would always make her feel better. One day, Elizabeth and her family moved far away by covered wagon. The quilt was not packed with the other quilts because it was wrapped around Elizabeth. Elizabeth's father built a new house in the woods and a new toy horse for her. Everything was new except for the quilt. Her mother wrapped her in the quilt and rocked her and tucked her in bed. Although Elizabeth felt at home again under the quilt nothing else was quite the same. Everything was new except the quilt.

When Elizabeth grew up and had her own family, she put her old very used quilt away in the attic and forgot about it. A mouse found the quilt and had her babies in it. The babies grew up in the quilt's stuffing and ate one of the falling stars. Next, a raccoon found the quilt and loved it so much she hid an apple in it.

Eventually, a cat found the quilt and curled up in it softly purring and fell sound asleep. One day, a little girl named Amelia was searching for her cat and she found the quilt. Amelia picked it up and wrapped it lovingly around herself. She took the quilt to her mother and asked her to please fix it. Her mother smiled and sewed up the holes, put in new stuffing, and stitched on new stars with long tails.

One day the little girl and her family moved far away. They traveled in a car over many miles of highways. They unpacked their things in a new house but nothing was quite the same. Everything was new except for the quilt. Amelia's mother lovingly wrapped her in the quilt and rocked her to sleep and tucked her in bed. Amelia felt at home again under the quilt.

To every thing there is a season and a time to every purpose under heaven.

Ecclesiastes 3:1

AMELIA ANNE BARTHOLOMEW

KeVondra Mack

She was my mother at school
She was beautiful in her own special way
She had a heart filled with love
She had a smile that lit up the room
She had the hair of an angel

Now, I only know her as memories
I know she has big beautiful wings
Brighter than the sun
I know she feels perfect in her new home
Up in the clouds in the big blue sky
Amelia Anne Bartholomew
I do love you

P O E T I C E U L O G Y

SHANNON LITTLE

Please do not cry because I'm not here
Please do not shed a tear
For I am still in your heart
And that is where I'll always be
I will always love you
It is true
I am not truly gone
I will live on in your memory
I miss you all
But now I'm soaring in the sky
And this will be our final goodbye

W H E N   I   D I E

JADE' SUBBER

The day I die, don't be sad
Don't weep and mourn
Actually, be glad
Not glad because I've died
But because of where I'm going
To my Father's house
Is where I'm going
Being on earth was only part one
Of my life
Now, I'm in the everlasting part
Talk to me through your prayers
And think about me all the time
I love you all now and forever
Love me back
When I'm gone
I won't ever come back

CHANGE

We must become the change we want to see.

Mahatma Gandhi

MS. KATHERINE PATRICK'S CLASS

The dogmas of the quiet past are inadequate to the stormy present. The occasion is piled high with difficulty; and we must rise with the occasion. As our case is new, so we must think anew and act anew.

Abraham Lincoln

INAUGURAL POEM

AYANA MCKINNEY CLAXTON

Change is good
Change is great
Change is joy
Change isn't hate
Change is fun
Change is cool
Change isn't a fool

Change is a wonderful event that happened to
this world on January 20, 2009. President Barack
Obama is going to change the world!

CHANGE

IRVIN DELGADO

President Obama will make change in the United States of America. We will be a great country. He will change the world because he's the 44th president. He won't give up on hope and freedom. He's part of a historic day. He will bring change. It's an important day for my parents and me because we might have a successful future. He has promised change.

CHANGE

ALEXUS MARTIN

Change is something we all do
Change happens to me
To you
But nothing is like the change today
We have a black president
Hurray! Hurray!
This event is really, really big
It will be in the history books
I am a part of history
I think this is very cool
This is bigger than me
I know change is really great
This is the best thing ever
Hurray! Hurray!
I will never forget this day
One more time
Hurray! Hurray!

CHANGE

PEY

Change is what we wanted all this time
I'm glad we have it now
But sad we did not have it before
President Obama brought change
Change, Change, Change
Is what America
Is
Hungry for
Change

CHANGE IS
BARACK OBAMA

PAYTIN BROWN

Change, Change, Change
Is what we want
Change, change, change
Is what we'll get
Barack Obama
Is the first
African American President
He made a difference
All it takes is
Courage, strength, and
A belief in yourself

CHANGE IS
BARACK OBAMA

GABRIEL EPPS

It's time for a change
It's no game
Our nation will change
Because of this time in history
Change has begun
More will come
Yes, it's true
He is our President
Barack Obama
He will change America
Dr. King's dream has become a reality
Both men brought change
It's time for a change
It's no game
Our nation will change because of this
Time in history
We will change

CHANGE

LaMonica Souter

Change is a good word
The word change is a word people use a lot
The change of the seasons
Change is all around us
Barack Obama is going to change our nation
Change is good
Everyone should change
Barack Obama becoming our first black president is special
This day will change my life
When I'm older
I'll tell my children
My children will tell their children
Barack Obama is going to change our future

CHANGE

MALEIK GATEWOOD

Change can be a good thing
Barack Obama as President of the United States
Is a good thing
Change will help the United States
Get back on top
It will help the economy get better
Change will help us get more jobs
I hope change can get everyone back on the right track

CHANGE

JEROME FOSTER, JR.

No more problems
No more bad things
Like Barrack Obama said, it's time for a change
He wants change for every child
A new president
A brand new style
This will make history
For a long, long, long time
If I had one
I would put him in a shrine
I knew he would win the votes
I'm glad it's a black president
It's something new
I will stop talking now
Because I'm through

CHANGE

DEANGELO BROOKS

Change requires getting along
To the point where you are the master of your ability
A little is better than none
Heaven helps some
Just give a penny
That will do
And change will come to you

CHANGE

MARLOS CRUMB

When I think of America
I think of many words
Free, life, free will, and free birds
When you think America has gone down the drain
And it will never be the same
Keep hope
Because we could expect change

Changes

WILLIAM ORELLANA

Change means improvement
And change means hope
This year, Obama hopes to bring improvement
This will cause a big, big, movement?
Change brings hope
Hope for the future
Change requires leadership and responsibility
Obama has the ability to bring a change
We can believe in

CHANGE

EARON GREEN

Obama is finally president
He is the meaning of change
In the economy, you know
We need a change
So, Obama, please do your job
Change
Change

CHANGE

JEFFERY UGWUANI

For the past hundred years change has come to America. However, one thing didn't change, the Presidents. Yes, we do change presidents every four years but the race did not change. In the past, one race has run the government.

One young man named, Barack Obama from Kenya in Africa has changed the nation. Barack Obama had a white mom from Kansas and a dad from Kenya who was black. Barack Obama was a Senator from Illinois. He ran against Senator McCain for president. Senator McCain made a lot of hurtful campaign remarks but Barack made more promising campaign remarks and ads.

The night of the election, everyone's hearts were jumping, their bodies shaking, and tears were shed when people finally heard what happened. Barack Obama had won the election. Everyone was jumping around because change had come to America. We all knew that this was a glorious day.

Black people all over the nation saw the glorious event. Even people from Kenya, Ghana, and even Nigeria were jumping and dancing. Barack became our 44th president and now is doing his job as our president.

He may not be able to cure the economy because it will take time. With everyone's help and support people can change this nation.

Yes, we can change America!

Change

ANONYMOUS

Change is all around us
We have our first African American President
Global warming
High gas prices
Earthquakes
Wars
Bombings
All of these events are changing our way of life
And, this new president
Thinks he can change it all
But, again, will we have a great fall?
We don't know if the United States
is going to change or not
I guess we will just have to ride it out

CHANGE

JESSICA

People come and people go
Today, I wrote this poem to let you know
Now that Obama has arrived
New jobs will come so we can survive
Back when we had Bush
We had nothing to do
Now that we have Obama
Things are made new
Obama will give us new jobs
And a new opportunity
Our economy will slowly rise
Now there will be a change
Everything will be better

CHANGE

SARAH MUFTI

At first black people didn't have rights
But now they are treated just like whites
Some people say that change is difficult
Some people say that change is bad
Change might even make some people mad
But after the way things have been
Everything will end with a grin

CHANGES

MERCHANT DOYLE

Rain, snow, or sleet
Change will come
It won't happen fast
But change will come
Presidents can make the nation good
Presidents can make the nation bad
A new president is in the White House
This president must make the economy better
It will take awhile
But I believe this President will help the economy
I believe change will come to the nation

CHANGE

KEANNYI WILSON

We needed a change
Someone out there needed to make a change
And then he came
Barack Obama came and made a change
A big change
To help our community
He made all of us smile
Including Martin Luther King
He is smiling down
Obama made the dream come true
Barack, you made the dream come true
Thank you
God bless

CHANGE

JASMINE BELL

Obama's going to get in the White House
And change our life
High gas prices
That's about to change
Layoffs, low pay, short hours
No problem, because a change has come
Our very first African American President
It's amazing after all these years
It's so unbelievable
Our eyes are filled with tears
After all these years
A change has come

CHANGE

KELSEY WEST

Change is a precious word
The name is musical
And you can sing
Change is what we need
Change is what we the people will bring
Change is what Barack Obama will bring

CHANGE

TAYLOR MOORE

Here we are
Staying focused and moving on
God has blessed us so
I'm not letting unfair people become my foe
Obama is our 44th President
A long way home

CHANGE

KIARRA HAYSLETT

Change is everything we need
We are getting it soon
Obama is a good thing
Change is just what we need
The world is getting ready for good
Barack Obama is what the world needs
The economy is so bad
We wish we had never let it get so bad

CHANGE

TATYANA L. GARRETT

Change is what we want
Change is what Obama is giving to us
Change is everything important
It takes everybody to make a change
Change
Change
We got to earn it
Obama, Obama
He is my change
We all can make a big change in life

CHANGE

BOBBY SCURLOCK

There was a time in our history
When the white and black were segregated
Instead of integrated
There was a time
When it was unheard of blacks
Living in a white neighborhood
There was a time when
We could not drink out of the white
Water fountains
Or eat at the white restaurants
Now it has changed

CHANGE

GAVIN GENTRY

This is a time for change
Change is to make some things different or right
President Obama has made that change
I believe this is the greatest historical moment
In my life
I think he will do a wonderful job
During the next 4-8 years in office

CHANGE

KEIRRA

Obama has created change for America
Now that I have seen what black people can do
I've decided to change my attitude
And decided to change my actions
And my community
And stop littering

CHANGE

MALIK JACKSON

I think that change is very good
Everyone will change at some point

CHANGE

BRANDON WRIGHT

After all these years
We have a change
We have been waiting and waiting and waiting
I'm glad that we have Obama
Welcome home

CHANGE

MARQUETTE MURDOCK

Time for a change
We have gone through so much pain
Now we are in the game
We will go so far
I'm so happy for Obama
That he won
Obama is so nice

CHANGE

BRANDON H

Obama saw that it was time for a change
Change means no violence
No drugs
No nonsense
I hope people live a good life
And do right
I hope gas goes down
Do right
Not wrong

CHANGE

ANEASEY LAYDEN

It's time or a change
Our old President was lame
Obama doesn't have time for this drama
He has a wonderful wife
I pray they can make it through life
I hope that his children grow up to be
Just like their dad
And not be bad
Obama is my inspiration
My idol
My superstar
I hope he teaches
Young boys to pull up their pants
And act like men

CHANGES

QUINCY PUGH

It's time for a change
Someone new is coming in this game
It's time for a new day
It's time for a change
President Obama do your thing
Soon, everybody will sing Obama
It's time for a change
Obama is the true name
McCain is so lame
Obama is a real man
Now, he will stand up and say
It's time for a change

CHANGE

RAVEN LYONS

Change is about a new you
Change is about a new President
Change is about a new year
A new everything

CHANGE

IESSHIA THOMAS

It's time for a change
Today, it is here
Obama is our President
He will always be near
He's going to make a change for me
He's going to make a change for you
So, we can get strong
And become what we dream to be

CHANGE

DYLAN THOMAS

Barack Obama is our new President
Change is on its way
We the people believe in it
He checked in the office
He'll be the best he can be
Some of us believe in him

CHANGE

KALEN IVERY

Change is what we need
We don't need people in our face
Making it harder
We need Obama
He is everything we dreamed of
I'm tired of people yelling McCain
It is time for a change
Yes, we can make it happen

INAUGURATION POEM

JOSHUA KUYKENDALL

Millions and millions of people lined the streets
All came to see a grand treat
They braved the bitter cold
For they were young and old

Everyone is yelling, *yes we can*
Obama is our man
We watched at school
As we sat on our stool

CHANGE

DEQUAN BROWN

Roses are red
Violets are blue
If you change
I will too

CHANGE

BRANDON ADAMS

Obama has caused change
Obama has made history
He is our first black President
We want everyone to be treated equal
That was the dream of Martin Luther King
It has come true

Ms. Deborah Dyson's 8ᵀᴴ Grade Language Arts Class

OBAMA'S TIME 2 SHINE

SHAKYRA BOHANON

His name is Obama

He is black

I know a lot of people don't like that

He is a man with lots of pride

Obama won, McCain can go on a joy ride

In January, he will be on his way to the white house

Making if official

And certified

That this is it

He stands for what is right

Join in the fight

Obama, Obama, a successful man

He is Obama

Yes, he can

Obama deserves to be honored

It's Obama's time to shine

CHANGE

DERRIUS WELLS

When Barack Obama came into the game
He didn't have a name
Now, he's president
He has all the fame
When he was growing, he did well in school
He didn't walk around with his pants sagging like a fool
He worked real hard for what he got
He didn't walk around throwing up gang signs
So he could get shot
He graduated first in his class
He only went with who was smart, not fast
Now he's president
Gas has gone down
It's Barack Obama's turn now
It's time to pass down the crown
Every meeting he went to, he was never late
Every event that came up, he would participate
Now, Barack Obama is President
It's time for a change
Everything that was messed up
Is about to change

BARACK OBAMA TO THE WHITE HOUSE

BOBBI WILLIS

November the 4th is my time of year

To hear Obama speak as we cheer

Vote for Barack

I'm sure you'll be proud

As we stand here cheering loud

The heavens open up

The dream pours out

As a new leader emerges

There is little room for doubt

Glorious, an American legacy

Days, moments, and eras presenting themselves

A time most thought

Their eyes wouldn't see

Wait until the day finally arrives

As we watch all the joy

Adults celebrating

Children saying, *oh joy!*

Barack Obama going down in history

Get ready

Get ready

A new beginning

Is on its way

CHANGE

ANONYMOUS

Change
It is a big thing
People do not understand change
A lot of things change
People just cannot believe it
Change
Is what Obama
Wants for the Kids of the USA

CHANGE

QUINCY PUGH

It is time for change
Someone new coming in the game
No shame
It is time for a new day
To say it is time for a change
Obama, do your thing
Soon, everybody will sing Obama
It's time for a change
Obama is a real man
Now, he will stand and say
Time for a change

BARACK'S THE ONE

JESSICA JOSEPH

Such a wonderful man that stands with pride
Barack Obama
A man that engages in hard solid thinking
Barack Obama
He has a shoulder that we can cry on
Barack Obama
The one that isn't afraid to show his
intelligence when speaking
Barack Obama
Hopefully, he can help us succeed
Barack Obama
Right now
He is what we really need
Barack Obama

BARACK OBAMA

JOSHUA MCBRIDE

Barack Obama worked very hard
He lived in Hawaii
He is somewhat of a star
During his campaign
He traveled to many states
He walks tall like a giant
He is now President
Of this great Nation

OUR PRESIDENT, OBAMA

DANIELLE ROHLEDER

We asked for a leader
One smart and wise
Now we have a president
Who can see through the eyes of the needy
We needed this man so much in our lives
He can stop the sobs and cries
We won't see anymore gangs at night
Obama will make everything right
It doesn't matter if you are
Black or white
As long as our president is brave
Obama is brave
Obama is strong
Now we know
Nothing will go wrong
He will fight for the USA
No matter what other countries say
Go Obama!

CHANGE

ALEXIS HANSBROUGH

Barack Obama is such an inspiration to me
I can't wait to get a chance to see
What he has planned for this year
He is our protector
As they say on the Tom Joyner Morning Show
We are black and yes we are back
Barack Obama, Michelle Obama, and even
the Obama girls have an effect on me
He is going to make a change
You just wait and see
When he became President
It was a moving sight
You could see the tears roll down my face
My President is black

BARACK OBAMA

AVIANCE BUTLER

Obama the President
The first black man
If he can do it
I know I can
To see him make a speech
And tell what he can do
Makes me want to go
And run for class president too
Obama can accomplish a lot of things
I know this world is in a big mess
I know he can cure it with no stress
I have faith and so does he
This world can become better
If we believe
Obama can make a change in my life
He can do it
I've never had so much faith
Obama, the President
The first black man
If he can do it
I know I can

BARACK OBAMA

SHUNICE N. REED

Yea, it's Barack Obama
You know his name
Glad he's in office
Because *it's time for a change*
It was good
He was elected President
Now, you can understand what his speech meant
It is not because he is a black man
It is because he came and took a stand
Obama took a stand
For what he knew we needed
Barack is a powerful and encouraging man
Because of his race
People didn't listen to his powerful sayings
I'm glad Obama was elected in 2008
This year's election is the first time
I paid attention
This is our President
Barack Obama

T H A T ' S   J U S T
W H A T   W E   D O

GARRISON DEANDREA

We saw him honestly
But we didn't believe because
That's just what we do
We never change our attitudes because
That's just what we do
Ignorant opinions became wretched
We didn't care because
That's what we do
We can never whole heartedly believe because
That's just what we do
A new way of doing, seeing, and feeling is here
Because the change is here
Obama

Victory for Obama

Betty Okongo

Let me tell you abut a man
A man who made history
We thought it wasn't possible for this victory
He proved us wrong
He proved to be a great man
He made the impossible
Possible
A great man
He had the courage to do
What most of us thought couldn't be done
Barack Obama

THE CHANGE

DONEVIN SMITH

Barack Obama won
Now all is well and done
So now, we can go home and rest
While Obama does the rest
We sit and wonder
What he will do
Will he sit like all the rest or
Take us all the way through
Through the good and the bad
The hard and the good times
We all know what he will do
He won't let us down
He will fight for what is right
And take us all the way
He is honest and courageous
He is our President
He will lead us all the way through
That's what he will do

WE WILL MAKE IT

KATRINA M

Barack Obama has been elected President
A lot of people think of him as an inspiration
He has encouraged me to strive for the best
We no longer can say, "I can't because
I am African American."
Obama has said, "Things will become
worse before they get better."
Just knowing that he is our President
Has put a smile on my face
Through all the hated threats and lies
Barack Obama has made it
People are being laid off, but we still make it
Through this election, I have learned so much
To keep my head held high no matter what happens
I know now that I can be anything
Maybe even the
President of the United States

BARACK OBAMA
A ROLE MODEL

DEION JONES

If I had a chance to vote
I would vote for Obama
He is full of character and encouragement
I couldn't have voted, but my mom should have gone
His intelligence is very amazing
I just hope he can do the right thing
I know he will be a great President
And, hopefully he will be again
I want to be like him definitely
But, I will truly have to study
I would like to go to Yale
Barack Obama making history
Is like a fairy tale

BARACK OBAMA MADE HISTORY

DAPHNE SEGREE

Barack Obama is our new President
He holds the United States in his hands
We hoped for a change
Change is on the way
We took the time to cast our votes
History was made on November 4, 2008
As we sit and wait to see what comes our way
I never thought we would have an African American
In the White House
Sometimes, you have to wait and see
We can't rush what our President will do
When he walks into the *new* House

BARACK OBAMA

KEIRAH SLACK

Barack Obama is the new President
Everyone is enthusiastic for a change
To make life better
Help us regain strength
Is there hope for this man?
Or will our country stay the same?
I have hope that life will get better
It's amazing that he's here
He's here to make things right
Such determination and leadership
Those are the traits our President needs
The supporters of Barack Obama
Are ready for a change
Obama can make a change
If he puts his heart into the work
Are you ready for a change?

BARACK
OBAMA CAN

CORDARIUS RAYNER

Barack Obama is the President-elect
He is going to change our nation
The first black president in history
Barack Obama is a successful man
We will see America move
Obama will show us how to improve
Some people are judging him because of his color
Obama is here to change the economy
Give Obama some time
Yes, Barack Obama can

BARACK OBAMA

MARIAH PILLOWS

Barack Obama is a strong black man
He always says, "We can…we can."
He sees the opportunity
And talks to us through the news and television
He is the perfect President
I believe he is heaven sent
Barack Obama is a strong black man
He always says, "We can…we can."
He talks about the problems we face
And makes us believe there is a better place
He visits different cities
And talks about opportunities
Barack Obama is a strong black man
He always says, "We can…we can."

BARACK OBAMA

BRANDON WEATHERSPOON

Barack Obama is a great man
He deserves to be president
Not just because he is black
He can make a change
Now that he is president
I know that he is going to make our country
A better place to live
A great weight was lifted from some people's shoulders
There is going to be a change

OUR 44TH PRESIDENT

TYRA ISAACS

History has been made

Change will soon rise up

He will solve problems with compromises and pride

People said it would never happen but

Our President is African American

He will always be remembered for the change he will make

History has been made

Our USA remains great

BARACK OBAMA

BRITTANY BETHEL

Now life is grand
Voting for Barack Obama can give you fame
Once you go for Barack
You can't go back
He's smart as a tack
He will ease our fears
He will be the one to stop our tears
He's the one and only
He's Barack Obama
Barack Obama is
As American as apple pie

THE NATION

GERALD SANFORD

The nation is happy
The nation is sad
The world is nice
The world is mean
It's full of darkness
It's full of light
Who will be our silver knight?
To protect us from the evil knight
The police are trying, but that isn't enough
Barack is running
I hope he wins
He will change the nation
He is black and intelligent
And soon will be our President

WHAT'S REALLY IMPORTANT?

JESSICA JOSEPH

Presidential elections are complicating our life
Most of the time, they're not as fun as they seem
We never really understand until we watch the debates
Yea, I know they're kind of banal
Then, we must decide
Obama for President! The whole crowd roars
The crowd behaves like wild bears
and lions fighting for a feast
Obama! No, McCain!
But no one really sees
The Nations in trouble and it will soon die
The government is starting to seem like one big lie
Well, I'm tired of this
I'm not going to tell you who I think should win
But, with his help, we could probably get this straight
Come on, United States, it's time for a change!

MUSINGS

Mrs. Dyson's Students

SUMMER TIME

TYRA ISAACS

Summer is a time of change
Summer is a time of leisure and of play
Summer is a time of sleepovers
And a time for sleeping in
Summer is a time of eating ice and of eating ice cream
Summer is a time just for me

My Ode to Education

Tyra Isaacs

I pledge to do my best
I pledge to strive harder than the rest
On some days, I feel like giving up
I pledge to do my best
Even on those days that I feel like I have given my all
I pledge to do my best
My loyalty to education is what will secure my future
For that, I pledge to do my best

MUSIC IS EVERYTHING

TYRA ISAACS

Music is my life
Music is the laughter that makes me cry
Music is the thing that changed my life
Music is the happiness I feel inside
When I play music
It is my everything
When I'm down
Let it turn me around
Whatever I am feeling
Let the music take over
Let it wash though me
Let it undo me
Turn the music up loud and
Sing it all around
Just sing your soul out and
Show everyone what you're all about
Music is my life
Music is the laughter that makes you cry
Music is the happiness I feel inside when I play
Music is my life

BAND

GERALD SANFORD

Band is fun
Band is cool
You can earn a college scholarship
You can make money
Through this journey
You have to read music

Friends will come and go
Some will hurt you
Some will steal
Don't let go of your pride
Keep your head alive
Band is fun
Band is cool
Hold your head high
See your way through
You can be a legend

CECILIA LUNA

I sometimes think about myself
And how I might be better off
Though I have a hard life
I can still do better in life
At times, I study for the best
But, at times, I just become one less
I know that I have to stop and pay attention
So I can be someone with high expectations
I can improve in school
But, I have to do what I have to do
And, looking at kids with no respect for themselves
Makes me want to get a mirror for them
To realize it
I am realizing that I need to try harder
For I am better than that
And, I will try to accomplish my work

DR. PRECIOUS BOYLE
SOCIAL STUDIES

TODAY

THOMAS NORTON

Today is the Big Day
What we all have waited to see
What we thought was impossible
Has finally come to be
Barack Obama, our first African American President
I believe in this moment
He was truly God sent
There was a change of power on January 20
It was a very cold day, but one that we will remember
He moved his family to a new address
As our Nations' problems may cause him stress
He gave a powerful speech
As he spoke to the world
To encourage us all: men, women, boys, and girls
I wish him well
As he leads our Nation
We must do our part for future generations
President Obama, the man for this time
I will pray for him
As he lets his light shine
As he climbs the mountains

Set before him
I know he will reach the top
No matter how grim
Yes we can, yes we can
He reminds us we must
But, I believe we can only do this work
If in God we put our trust

1 - 2 0 - 0 9

BRITTNEY ADU

On this historic day
We all will never forget
Barack Obama won our votes
And this, we won't regret
He is truly an amazing man
He makes his points with *Yes we can*
The Inauguration brought joy
To men, women, and every girl and boy
A legacy that will be very fine
On the day 1-20-09

1 - 2 0 - 0 9

BREANNA ROBERSON

This day is very special
This day is guaranteed
To be the most special day
We might ever see

I heard his words
His speech of change
Thinking in my head
He's America's next page

He unites the people
In every way possible
He just goes to show you
That nothing is impossible

1 - 20 - 09

ALEXIS SMITH

Barack Obama and I are honest
We do things just because of the children
We both play basketball
We both believe in the same principles
We are heroes to people
I am here to say
Barack Obama is my hero
Barack took the oath to be President today
I would have never been able to do that
He gets to do many things
He has the codes to all weapons now
Everyone, including me, trusts him
We believe he will protect us
These are my thoughts
When I watched
The Inauguration of Barack Obama

He's the One to Make Change

CAMERON DANDRIDGE

Barack Obama is the one to make change
He came out on top about John McCain
Barack Obama the dream has come true
The first African American President
Greater change is to come
Barack Obama will serve us all
The 44th to plead the oath on 1-20-09
The First African American President
Barack Obama
Change is to going to come

1 - 20 - 09

TYLER SIMMONS

On 1-20-09, the inauguration of the
44th President will occur
On 1-20-09, history will be made
On 1-20-09, Barack will make his address
On 1-20-09, Michelle will be the First Lady
On 1-20-09, Sasha and Malia will become America's Angels
On 1-20-09, the Obama's will live in the White House
On 1-20-09, Barack will be the first black President
On 1-20-09, I will see my possibility

January 20, 2009

JAMAURA MAYHUE

The experience was great
Sorry that I couldn't be there
I surely watched it on TV
Barack Obama is President

It was an important moment in history
I believe African Americans made history once again
It is electrifying that I could share
that experience with all races
Barack Obama is President

I think America is going to be different from now on
From the way we travel
To the way we are being educated
I truly believe that it's time for a change
Barack Obama is President

MRS. GIVINIA CAUSEY
SEVENTH GRADE CLUE

TCAP BLUES

MIGUEL ESCAMILLA

I went to school to take the TCAP
I was all worried
I went to school to take the TCAP
I was all worried
Didn't want to test, but I had to
I hurried and scurried
To get the test over with
I hurried and scurried
To get the test out of the way
Everybody was ready, except me
Oh my gosh, here it comes
Ooo ooee eeee
Boy, her it comes
I might be ready, or maybe not
Tell the teacher
I might be ready, or maybe not
I believe I will do badly
Tell the teacher
Oh boy, tell the teacher
I might be ready, or maybe not

TCAP BLUES

ANONYMOUS

I got the TCAP Blues
And I don't know what to do
I study and study all day and all night
And I study with all of my might
To try and get advanced on that test
On TCAP day we are all nervous
Hoping that we know the answers for the test
But if we don't
We make an educated guess
We eliminate answers to find one that
answers the question best
All TCAP week in class
It's super quiet
'Cuz, we're all focused so we can be advanced
But when it's over
We are even more glad
After TCAP's over
The pressures all over
Oh, but this thinking ahead
Has made me have that TCAP Blues again

I GOT THE TCAP FLU

DENZEL COOPER

I got the TCAP Flu
Don't call it Blue
But the TCAP Flu

In April it comes along
To my home
You year this sick song
We study hard for this crazy test
Trying to do our best
We get no rest
Man, who would have guessed?
I blame it on Tennessee
For putting this dirty, dirty Flu on me

I got the TCAP Flu
Don't call it Blue
But the TCAP Flu

You take this Devil Test
It leaves you in a complete mess
You finally get some rest
English, Science, Social Studies and Math
Your brain stinks so much it needs a bath

I got the TCAP Flu
Don't call it Blue
But the TCAP Flu

TAKING TCAP

SHANNON LITTLE

Taking TCAP
It's no fun
It's no fun
You have to study
And get a good night's sleep
Trying hard
To get the best grade possible
To get the best grade possible
It can cause a lot of stress
But when it's over
You can take a nice long rest

ODE TO MY MOTHER

SHANNON LITTLE

Ode to my mother
Who is young and bright
Ode to my father
Who is always right
Ode to my brothers
Who love me so
Ode to my cousins
Who I barely know
Ode to my friends
Who are always there
Ode to my grandparents
Who always care
Ode to my uncles
Who hold me tight
Ode to my aunt
Who would be there all night
Ode to my family
Who I love so much
Ode to my pets
Who I love just as much
I really care for them
Each and every one of them

Me and my Boyfriend

Rachel Wright

Me and my boyfriend
Had to break up
Oh, you get the point
Well, I shouldn't be grieving
But, he shouldn't be deceiving
Anyway, it's time to move and play

LOOK AT ME

DANIELA GARCIA

Look at Me
And you can see who I am
A free-spirited child of God
With love in my heart
And thoughts in my mind
My looks don't define
But they tell a story
My hair curls in waves
Like the ocean

LIVING

MIGUEL ESCAMILLA

Living is a blessing
Because you never know
If you'll be alive
To witness the next show

Some people feel invincible
But others fear all day
Because they're not sure
If they'll live 'til May

I always thank God for letting me live
And not letting me die
Because if I pass
Many people will cry

I cannot predict the future
But there's one thing I know
There is another day
For you to witness the show

FAMILY TRADITIONS

JAMAURA MAYHUE

Peace
We gather for a dinner together
Happily

Love and Care
Everyone laughing, Joking and having fun
No one arguing like a bunch of animals
Everybody enjoying the dressing, turkey, and pie
Crescent moon shining brightly in the sky
Hearing only crickets chirping

Love and Care
We gather for a dinner together
Happily

TRADITION

TYLER SIMMONS

Be thankful for your blessings instead of your crosses
Be thankful for your gains instead of your losses
Be thankful for your joy instead of your woe
Be thankful for your friends instead of your foes
Be thankful for your smile instead of your tears
Be thankful for your courage instead of your fear
Be thankful for your full years instead of your lean
Be thankful for health instead of your wealth
Be thankful for God instead of yourself
If you're not thankful for these things
I'm sorry to say
But at least be thankful for Thanksgiving Day

FAMILY REUNION

BREANNA ROBERSON

Every August
Of every year
My family comes in
From far and near

My Aunts and Uncles
Give big hugs
While my parents and I
Return the love

Some of my cousins
Come to tell me what's been going on
While my other cousins
Sit and talk on the lawn

I take the cutest pictures
Of my whole family
And as I show them off
They gather around to see

We sit around and eat
And talk with good times
Moments like this make me happy
To know that this family is mine

If only my grandparents were here
To see how much our family has grown
And sometimes I wish
We never have to go home

LOOK AT ME

D A N I E L A   G A R C I A

Look at me
And you can see who I am
A free-spirited child of God
With love in my heart, and thoughts in my mind
My looks don't define, but they tell a story
My hair curls in waves, like the ocean
It lies on my shoulders and models itself dauntlessly
Look at me
And you can see who I am
A free-spirited child of God
With love in my heart, and thoughts in my mind
My looks don't define, but they tell a story
My frame, petite and small but strong and able
And my hands fragile and soft
With fingernails painted in bright colors
Look at me
And you can see who I am
A free-spirited child of God
With love in my heart, and thoughts in my mind
My looks don't define, but they tell a story
Legs long and free, running and sprinting toward life

Look at me
And you can see who I am
A free-spirited child of God
With love in my heart, and thoughts in my mind
My looks don't define, but they tell a story
Look at me!

ODE TO MY MOUTH

DANIELA GARCIA

You talk and talk
A never ending chat
I feed you daily
What would I do without you, Mouth?
Braces I have put into you
And bit your tongue many times
You still support me, dear old Mouth
You chew the food I put into you
Delicious or not
You speak two different languages
And tell many things to the world
What would I do without you, Mouth?

MY LIFE

DANIELA GARCIA

Born on a windy day
I guess I am special, yes you can say
I learned to say *daddy* first
Then *mommy* came along
After that, I could sing my first song
At three, I learned to read
Cute as a button, yes indeed
My coming to the United States later became
Learning a new language wasn't a game
First grade, I had to move
To a new school, not too far away
But, I was glad to not have to stay
Later on middle school came
And here I am today

MEMORIES

DANIELA GARCIA

Memories
Sitting on the porch
Munching on watermelon
Remembering those days
Where we could scream and play
Ah, such grand memories, I say
From wearing diapers to buying your first DC
Then having your first crush
And writing about him in your diary
Starting middle school
Then graduating high school the next day
Time passes by so quickly
Sitting on the porch
Munching on watermelon
Remembering those days
Where we could scream and play
Ah, such great memories, I say

JOSLYN WEATHERS

Joslyn
Independent
Outgoing, Cheerleader
Intelligent human being
That's Me

M O M

JAYLEN BOGA

Mom
She is sweet
She is loving
Her heart is where
I am
Love

WHO WILL CRY FOR THE LITTLE WOLF?

ALEXA PANAMENO

Who will cry for the little wolf?
That wanders the forest all alone
With nothing but memories
Of a mother who is long gone

A too familiar battering sound
Sends his heart to a quicker rate
He begins to run as fast as he can
Ignoring the tired muscles that groan and ache

Running for his life
Is something he does on a daily basis
Along with many other animals
Who play the targets in these deadly chases?

Dashing through the forest in zigzagged lines
Afraid to slow down
Though the helicopter is now far behind
When stopping to catch his breath
The wolf hears ear splitting bangs, and a piercing cry
The pup begins to calm down
He made it this time

So who will cry for the little wolf?
No one
That's who
But if we really cared
We'd do something about slaughter
Wouldn't we?

MAGIC WORLD

ALEXA PANAMENO

The great and wonderful world of magic
Will leave you in awe and wanting to know more

From the tiniest pixie in a tree
To the mighty dragon that rules the sky
Trees dance and sway to the beat of the heart
Firefly shows light up star sprinkled nights
While the mermaid's song is heard for miles

Jewels better than any king's are found
Animals there roam free without a fear
Of being slaughtered or beaten to death

A place where worries can be forgotten
And stress is replaced by warm happiness
Oh, if only there was some kind of way
For the wind to bring that magic to our day

ODE TO THE INTERNET

ALEXA PANAMENO

The internet is one of the greatest things today
Anyone can use it
Use it at home for fun or for school
You can even use it to buy a new pool
Get on the internet and listen to music,
play games, and much more
As long as there's a computer around
You'll never be bored

While on the internet you can travel to different places
See new things
Meet new faces
You can also keep in touch with family and friends
Oh, the power of the internet
Really is the best

LETTERS TO SHARON DRAPER

DR. PRECIOUS BOYLE HOMEROOM

and

MS. SUSAN FERRARA'S LANGUAGE ARTS STUDENTS

Dr. Boyle inspired her homeroom students to read Sharon Draper's books. Our principal, Ms. Lisa Henry has arranged for Ms. Draper to visit Ridgeway Middle in 2010. The following letters express the students' joy of reading Ms. Draper's books.

Dear Ms. Draper:

I enjoyed reading your book series. The series was really entertaining. I'm not really the type that likes to read. Then, my teacher, Dr. Boyle made us read them. As I started to read your books, I thought that for once, reading was fun. Your books really touched me in a way that I thought reading could never do. The kind of books that you write, give directions in life that will help me in similar situations.

Those were just some things I wanted to let you know about your books. I admire you.

Before I end this letter, I wanted to ask you a couple of questions. What do you do before you start writing a book? Second, what do you do to come up with your ideas for books? How did you begin your career?

Thank you for your time.

Very truly,

Brieanna Neely

Dear Ms. Draper:

I enjoy reading all of your books because they connect to many youth. Your books are the best books ever about events that are happening in the present.

You write so many good books that I have to ask you some questions. How old were you when you found out that you wanted to be a writer? Who inspired you to become a writer? What is your favorite book? Finally, will you keep writing more books?

Ms. Draper, you have inspired me so much. You even inspired my cousin that lives in Germany and had never heard of you. I just want to say that I love your book; *November Blues* and that you are the best writer ever!

Sincerely,

Alexis Smith

Dear Ms. Draper:

I really enjoy reading your books. Whenever I have nothing to do, I just pick up one of your books. Although I have already read all of them, I enjoy reading them again. The *Hazelwood Trilogy* was the most amazing teen related story ever written.

My favorite story is *Forged by Fire*. I like it because it is so amazing. Reaching the climax of the story just made me want to continue reading and crying. I hope you will write more *Hazelwood Trilogy* books.

Yours truly,

Kayla Brodnax

Dear Ms. Draper:

I am a student at Ridgeway Middle, and I enjoy reading your books. My favorite book is *Darkness Before Dawn.* The reason I like this book is because Angel finished what her dad started.

How do you come up with such great ideas for books? Hopefully, you will publish many more good books.

Thanks for reading my letter. I hope you have a good time here at Ridgeway Middle.

Very truly yours,

Sydney McKinney

Dear Ms. Draper,

I have read your books: *Tears of a Tiger, Forged by Fire, Darkness Before Dawn* and now I'm reading *The Battle of Jericho.* Your books have taught me to do correct things at all times. You teach so many lessons about life.

Are all of your books based on true stories? Did the teenager in the story really die? Did that boy really kill himself? Was a little girl molested by a grown man? Did a young man really molest young girls who were between the ages of 15 and 18 years of age?

I wonder about these things because they are so sad and terrible. Before I was introduced to your books, I couldn't stand to read. I thought it was sort of useless. Because of you, I like reading. When I read your books, I feel everything and see everything that is happening. I love your books. You are my favorite author. I can't wait to see you when you visit my school. I have a lot of good questions for you to answer.

Yours truly,

Breonna Miller

Dear Ms. Draper:

I love your books. The first book I read was *Tears of a Tiger.* So far, it is the best. The saddest part of the book is when Andy committed suicide on his brother's birthday.

The other books I read are *Forged by Fire, Darkness Before Dawn, and Copper Sun.* These books were great, but not as good as *Tears of a Tiger.*

Those marvelous books inspired me very much. Now, I am writing books of my own. One of my books is called *Food: Friend or Foe.* Now, I would like to ask some questions. How old were you when you started to write? What inspired you to write? Are those books based on true stories?

Sincerely,

Dantaya Boyd

Dear Ms. Draper:

Your books are great! *Tears of a Tiger and Forged by Fire* made me cry. Your stories are very moving, and I have almost finished all of them. The books you have written connect to us because we talk *street* and use slang like the people in the books.

I want to know, How did you come up with ideas for your books? Did you have to research some things before you started writing or did it just come to you? What made you want to become an author? Did you ever want to be something else than an author? These are some of the questions that I have wanted to ask you.

I can't wait to get to meet you next year. Also, I've emailed you on your website once before. That's also where I saw most of your books that I haven't read yet. I'll get to them eventually.

Yours truly,

Jade' Subber

Dear Ms. Draper:

I love your books. At first, I was not too happy about reading, but as I began reading, I discovered it was the best book I'd ever read. Your books are interesting, not too dramatic, and humorous.

Thank you for writing these books.

Sincerely,

Quincey Byrd

Dear Ms. Draper:

I love your books. They are very interesting. *Tears of a Tiger* made me cry. It's actually my favorite book of yours. My homeroom teacher encouraged us to read all of your books. I really did not like to read, but your books quickly changed my mind about reading. I really enjoyed the books I chose to read from your selections.

Your books caught my attention because there were many characters in your books that I could relate. My favorite characters are Angel and Keisha. Angel is about my age and has been through a lot. Keisha is a very strong young lady. I have been through a lot like Angel and I consider myself very strong, just like Keisha.

Ms. Draper, you are very talented and I think you are the best writer ever. You made me open my mind to reading more and even writing short stories of my own.

Love,

Nukeya Murray

Dear Ms. Draper:

I have really enjoyed your books. My favorite book is *Forged by Fire*. I wanted to ask you a few questions: What college did you go to? How did you become a writer? What inspired you to write all of these books? Did any of the experiences you wrote about happen to people you know?

I will try to read all of your books. I am reading *Romiette and Julio.*

I really look forward to seeing you. I know you will have a great time visiting Ridgeway Middle School.

Sincerely,

Karlyn Lane

Dear Ms. Sharon Draper:

I am so excited. When I heard that you were coming to my school, it made my day. I have read every book in the Hazelwood Trilogy. Those are my favorite.

I can't wait until you come. When you come, I will sit in the front row to see you. I hope you can sign my book.

Truly your friend,

Jermarcion

Dear Ms. Draper:

I really enjoyed reading your books. They were the best books that I have ever read. My favorite was *Tears of a Tiger*. While reading your books, I can picture in my mind what is going on in the story. I cried when I was reading *Tears of a Tiger*. After each chapter, I wanted to keep reading. Your books show people how to deal with problems. Every book in the trilogy made me want to continue reading your books. Thank you for making an impact in my life.

Hope to see you next year!

Karen Scuife

Dear Ms. Draper:

I really enjoy reading your books. I never get bored while reading your books. They mostly talk abut real life issues. At first, I didn't like reading, but after reading my first Sharon Draper book, I started to read all the time.

Thank you for writing books that make me realize that life is too short not to live properly while I can. Your books also help me understand what a lot of people go through everyday. My favorite book is *Darkness Before Dawn.*

I just love your books.

Very truly yours,

Jamaura Mayhue

Dear Ms. Draper:

Your books are fantastic and filled with drama. I love your books. After reading the first paragraph of *Tears of a Tiger* I was drawn into the story. The more I read, the more I became curious. Once I finished the first book, I was eager to read more of your books. After I finished the trilogy, I realized that all of your books were great. You are a great author!

Very truly yours,

Tyler Simmons

Dear Ms. Draper:

Thank you for writing wonderful books! My class really likes them and we hope you write many more. My favorite was the sequel *Forged by Fire*. The characters in the book were very realistic.

I am very grateful for you coming to my school. It is a great honor to possibly meet a wonderful writer. Thank you again for writing fantastic books.

Sincerely yours,

Lily Wong

Dear Sharon Draper:

My name is Lammoris Jones. I'm in the sixth grade.

I'm writing to tell you that I love all of your books. One particular book stood out, *Tears of a Tiger.* I want to ask you some questions about the book. What inspired you to write this book? Why did Rob die? Why did Keisha and Andy have to break up with each other? Why did Andy have to kill himself? Why wasn't there more information on Gerald's stepdad beating him? Is Jeremy, who is still missed, the one who died in real life?

Congratulations on all of your awards.

Sincerely, lover of your books,

Lammoris Jones

Ms. Sharon Draper, will visit our school in November of 2010. Our students are preparing for her visit by reading many of her wonderful books. Our Library includes the following books:

Tears of a Tiger, Forged by Fire, Darkness before Dawn, Romiette and Julio, Double Dutch, Battle of Jericho, Copper Sun, November Blues, Fire from the Rock, We Beat the Street, and the *Ziggy and the Black Dinosaurs* series.

In our Professional Development Library we have the following books: *Teaching from the Heart and Not Quite Burned Out But Crispy Around the Edges.*

Ms. Mahalia Davis
Language Arts

WRITING PROMPT: DEVELOPING MY STUDENTS IS MY HIGHEST PRIORITY

RESPONSE WRITTEN BY:

AYANNA D. MARTIN

What I think Ms. Davis means by this statement is that one of her most important priorities is to help us learn. Also, I think it means that she wants to help us reach our full potential. You can really tell that Ms. Davis cares. It is really a powerful statement.

I like this statement because it shows that our teacher really cares about us and wants us to succeed. I believe that all teachers should care about their students and tell them. I believe students reflect their teachers and their work shows whether the teachers are doing a good job or not.

Also, in this statement it says this is her highest priority. That shows that Ms. Davis places us at the high end of her priorities. Students should be proud to have a teacher that cares. When students have a teacher that cares, we realize that we are blessed.

A teacher affects eternity; he can never tell where his influence stops.

1907 The Education of Henry Adams

Libraries allow children to ask questions about the world and find the answers. And the wonderful thing is that once a child learns to use a library, the doors to learning are always open.

Former First Lady Laura Bush

REFLECTIONS ON THE IMPORTANCE OF THE SCHOOL LIBRARY

A Library is important because I can read my favorite book in a cozy chair. I love the Library…love it and I always will. —Keannyi Wilson

A Library is important because there are many different types of books to read. You cannot talk in a loud voice. —Turika Taylor

A Library helps you to learn about history, how to draw, and even the history of sports. There are fairy tale books and computers too. Libraries can really help. —Jereme Foster

Reading is fun. At a Library, you can check out a book to read. —Alyssia Easley

You can learn to read better at your Library. I like going to the Library. —Terika Fifer

When you check out books at the Library, you have to bring them back in a matter of days. When you are in the Library, you have to be quiet. Libraries have so many amazing books. —Ramon Davis

Libraries help us increase our reading levels. —Samantha Beard

I love reading books. I always get into the books I read. I laugh, I cry, and I get mad. It's kind of amazing. Reading is Fun. —Taylor Moore

The Library is important because it is full of excitement. —Iesshia Thomas

I learned to be respectful to books. You have to bring the books back on time. —Erica Tate

The Library is important for learning and you also might find a great book. I like going to the Library because it's fun. —Dylan Thomas

My favorite chair in our Library is a restaurant booth. —Monteris Boyd

At the Library, you can look for your favorite artist or author. —Quincy Pugh

People love to read books that interest their brain. —Larry Ward

You will find new adventures in your library. —Raven Lyons

The Library is important because you always learn new things. Every time I go to the RMS Library I always want to learn something good. —Kalen Ivery

We read interesting books at our Library. —Bianca Carpenter

The things that you can do at a Library are unbelievable. If you don't know how to read, just ask. —Kelcy West

The Library is a clean, respectful, loving place to go. I love the Library. —Russell Turner

Because of the nice and helpful librarians, you can find almost any book you want. —Brandon Foster

You learn valuable things at your Library like how to keep track of your books and when to return them. I can't wait to check out a book. I hope to read 100 books in a year. —Lauryn Patterson

If we didn't have a Library, we would not be able to read or talk properly. —Brandon Adams

The Library is important because we can read, read, read, and read. —Sarina Hardy

The Librarian's name is Mrs. Hall. She is very kind. Mrs. Hall is always helping me when I come to the Library. When we need a book, she either tells us where the book is or we go to the computer card catalog. These are the reasons why I think the Library is helpful and also so important. —Deja Dickerson

The Library is important because you can learn very exciting information. The fantastic Library is fun, adventurous, and exciting. I love the Library. —Gabriel Epps

You can learn things you've never even thought you would ever learn. It's like a date with a book. The Library rocks! —Paytin Brown

Libraries can help you expand your knowledge and help you improve your reading. —William Orellana

The Library is important to me in a lot of ways. It is a way to calm down in a quiet area and read. —Kayla Harrison

The Library is very important. You can check out books, read books, work on the computer and learn new things. You can also learn where the books are located and where they belong when you take them off of the shelves. —Maleik Gatewood

You can read a book in a quiet area. The Library is the place to be. —Jeffery Ugwuani

A Library is important because of the exciting books and all of the things you can learn there. The Library keeps kids off of the streets, helps them not get hurt, and maybe going to jail. —KaDeja Hurt

MR. KEN GREENE'S
GENERAL MUSIC STUDENTS

MY VISION OF THE FUTURE

My Vision of the Future

Brianna Hayes

In my vision of the future, everything will be different. Cars will be fueled by trash instead of gas. We could solve a lot of problems like oil spills that kill lots of animals. People all over the world will contribute to the trash supply for cars so all of the trash we throw in land fills won't be a problem. Cars will also hover to help prevent traffic jams and car accidents.

School will only be for one hour. Students will attend 180 days of school. Kids will have more time to hang out with their friends. State tests will only be 30 questions for each subject. The tests will only last for one or two days.

The economy won't be in bad shape like it is now. Very, very, smart people will be in charge of all the money issues. No one will be out of a job and big pretty homes will not cost so much. All houses will be under $4000.

In my vision of the future, entertainment will be even better than it is now. Instead of 3D movies, there will be 4D movies. You will be up close to the actors and actresses.

People will not wear animal hides like they do now. If they wear animals, it must have died from natural causes. People who wear animal fur will have to use animals whose fur grows back, like sheep.

Finally, in my vision of the future, global warming will not be a major problem. Every two years, we will have a day when we don't use any energy at all.

My Vision of the Future

Daria Dorsey

My vision of the future is to have a better education for young kids like myself. Instead of going to school, we will stay at home and be taught by our parents.

Everyone will be able to see a concert even if you don't have a ticket.

The economy will be better because Barack Obama will make progress.

Our energy needs will be better because people will not have to fill their cars with gas anymore. They will just use water. We will have flying cars.

My Vision of the Future

Zach LaPrell

My vision of the future is that people will have fully electric cars that will charge in the amount of time that it takes to fill a car with gas. Instead of gas stations, we will have charging stations where we can charge our cars and pay very little.

The economy will eventually get better and people will be smarter about keeping our environment clean.

Education will be better because kids won't be disruptive. School will be more entertaining and have shorter school days. People will not be as lazy because exercising will be more fun.

My Vision

Justin Byrd

In my vision of the future, cars will be able to fly and the economy will be much better than it is now. There will not be worries about Global Warming and crime will make a dramatic drop. We will be a better country than we are now. There will be more available jobs, better education, and factories will be energy proficient. The future will be better because of Barack Obama. We will have more great presidents to come.

MY VISION OF THE FUTURE

ASYA WEST

My vision of the future is that we will have smart and active robots that can do whatever we want. They will do chores and other things that we don't want to do. The robot doesn't work on batteries or a charge. All it needs to work is garbage. It also goes to school and disguises itself as the student. The robot can be transformed into a human, dog, or anything you can think of creating. The robot will have special powers. The robot can even be transformed into an electric car and driven anywhere you want to go. The robots make their own money by catering to your needs. That's my vision of the future.

MR. KEN GREENE'S
GENERAL MUSIC STUDENTS

MUSIC

MUSIC AND MATH

SHARNIQUE SMITH

Music and math are similar in many different ways

I use both every single day

I use music and math at school, at home, and just having fun

Without music or math, I wouldn't be able to get anything done

MUSIC AND MY LIFE

SHARNIQUE SMITH

Music plays different roles in my life
It is included in many things I do

I like music because it is something my grandfather enjoyed
He was a great songwriter
I would like to learn more about his music

Music also helps me to concentrate and clear my mind

I love music for another reason
I love to dance
The different tempos and beats allow me to dance to the best
of my ability

Music is Everything to me

MUSIC

MARISSA SALLIE

The sound escapes and cares for me
As it wraps me in its comfort
Sad days, happy days, mad days
It's my medicine
The booming of the bass
Like a roaring thunder
It hears my cry
It pleases my soul
And gives me so much job

It's all I need
It runs my emotion and makes me whole
The only thing that can do all of this
That song
That sound
Creates that feeling

MUSIC MAKES ME FEEL

ELIESHA HOWARD

What is music?
A sound you just hear
A beat that makes you move

What is music?
Someone's voice that makes you chill
Someone's voice that makes you feel

What is music?
A polyrhythm with thousands of beats
It might sound so good
It makes you want to move your feet

What is music?
A stack of tempos
That you hear in your limo

What is music?
A bass you just bump
A note you just thump

What is music?
A blues, a rap
A song that makes you snap

MUSIC 2DAY

EBONE PAYNE

Music today in our world is a very big deal
I mean, that's how some people make a living today
If we didn't have music
Where on earth would we be?
I love music
It's my life
I use it when I'm in a bad mood
That's why music plays a big part in my life
Is music a big part in your life?
It's your choice

My Music...
Makes Me

Destiny Yarbrough

My music makes my world come alive
The beats and the rhythm can be slow or wild
When my heart is broken for whatever reason
Music makes it heal and keeps it from bleeding
When I'm in a bad mood because my whack haters
I can listen to music to make those thoughts come lata
Sometimes if I can't take my mind off my baby
I will listen to my music so I get off crazy
Music makes me fall in love
Music makes me fall out of love
But without my music
I wouldn't have a life
If I were a boy, music would be my wife
My music makes my world come alive

MUSIC IN THE LIGHT

DIANA ABU-OBEID

Music in the light
Shining so bright
I can sing from day to night
Soaring above the stars
Up so high
When I sing
The stars twinkle
When they twinkle
Up so high
I feel like a star
In the dark beautiful sky

MUSIC MOJO

ANONYMOUS

Music is all around the world
Music is what brings the girls
That's why the people love me when they hear me singing
They begin to start blinging
When I start singing
I can't stop
It's like a drug of hip hop
So let's stop, drop, and roll with music

MUSIC IS IMPORTANT TO ME

DAJA CAMPBELL

Music is important to me because it inspires me. It inspires me to listen more, to think about things that I have done and to do better than I did before. The kind of music I like is rap. I love it because some of it speaks about life and how people feel. It speaks about feelings. The sound of the voices tell us whether they are sad and lonely, happy or excited, or in love. These are the reasons that music is important to me. I love it.

The Legacy of Music

JEFFE' ROBINSON

In my eyes, music is loving and caring
I love music
Music is my life
It makes my mind wonder
It makes my mind wonder about things
Music is stories waiting to be revealed
Once the music is revealed
You can't stop listening
I listen to music both day and night
I love music

MISCELLANEOUS MUSINGS

WHEN DARKNESS LOVED ME

MARISSA SALLIE

I thought the dark gave me light
The pain gave me joy, but now it hurts
A black rose once cared and filled me with joy
And…passion and love
Now, it stabs me with thorns like knives
And kills me softly with every glance I take

A dark night once gave me light
Even in my sorrow
I thought it would bring me gladness, and yes it did
Now, it makes me blind
As I stumble through my life

I wish my darkness would serenade me again
And whisk me away
But it looks at me
And laughs
That hurts in every single way

TRUE TO MYSELF

QUISHA GRIFFIN

Being here and having blessings
Going to school and learning lessons
Doing the best that I can
Doing what the right person would
Not caring about what people think of me
Always standing up for the person I am and who I'll be

Believe in miracles if no one else will
Keep walking if someone I see is standing still
If I stop, it's just for a break
Any obstacle in the way, I will shake
There is no one that can shut me down
They will not turn me around

I will not give up, I will not give in
I'm not stopping until I win
Everything I've ever experienced, everything I've ever done
If I lose in a race, I will still be number one
Even when I'm angry, I'm happy that I'm here
Even if I go far away or I disappear

If I'm lost and don't know the way back home
I can always call for help on my phone
I can talk for hours and hours, so I won't feel alone
When I see the light, I know I'm there
No one Is under my skin or in my hair
If I don't make it today
If I don't make it tomorrow
I will not feel sorry for myself or feel sorrow

I will be true to myself and believe in me
Even if I'm not in the right place
Or not where I'm supposed to be
Wondering what point I'm trying to get across
In this world, I'm my own boss

LISTEN TO OUR CHILDREN

SHARON HALL

Stop and be quiet for a moment
Read their words
And hear their meanings
Learn
Our children's hopes, dreams, and
darkest fears are revealed
As they unlock the secrets held in their hearts
Pass through that door that is sometimes closed
And hear the parent's prayers for their
children, our nation, and our world
Our children have much information to share
Stop
Be still
Listen
We have much to learn

THE RMS TEACHERS THAT MADE THIS ANTHOLOGY POSSIBLE:

SUSAN FERRARA

DEBORAH DYSON

PRECIOUS BOYLE

KEN GREENE

KATHERINE PATRICK

MAHALIA DAVIS

GIVINIA CAUSEY

A SPECIAL THANK YOU TO MS. LISA HENRY, OUR PRINCIPAL OUR CAPTAIN!

Principals must live with paradox: They must have a sense of urgency about improving their schools, balanced with the patience to sustain them for the long haul. They must focus on the future, but remain grounded in today. They must see the big picture, while maintaining a close focus on details. They must be strong leaders who give away power to others.

Richard DuFour 1999